The Spider

 **Royston Cole**

11 Highoaks Road
Woolton
Liverpool L25 8RD

Phone: 0151 475 3904
Email: pcole@liv.ac.uk
Mobile: 0797 324 7821

Writer

 @RoystonCole

 RoystonCole65

Copyright © 2013 Royston Cole
All rights reserved.

ISBN: 1-4800-2157-1
ISBN-13: 9781480021570

The Spider

Royston Cole

2013

Dedication

For my family

1

The little pink ones were the worst.

Two of them; sitting there in the cereal bowl, trying to look innocent.

Bastards!

They had made his life miserable with their weird doings.

But now was not the time to worry about it.

With grimacing concentration, he tried not to worry about it—not now. For now, it was better that he focussed on the preparations.

So in went a purple diamond, the size of a thumbnail but nowhere near as tasty, and the lime green ovals: one, two, three, and four.

Next were a couple of friendly yellows. These would prevent a pink-purple clash and reduce the pain produced by the greens.

The end was in sight, and sprinkled in were five tiny whites; or maybe it was a sprinkling of seven, or ten tiny whites that had spent a moment on the palm of his hand before falling into the mix. They were so small that he had difficulty in seeing them individually, but a modest palmful was the measure that usually worked. The truth was that it didn't really matter how many tiny whites—five, seven, or twenty—for these were only saccharin.

Finally, a fistful of sugar-coated cornflakes, or this morning maybe two, and the steamy milk, poured from a saucepan that had just been rescued from the growling flames of an old and smelly gas stove.

The bowl was placed in the middle of a plastic tea tray. Next to it, a freshly laundered napkin was fastidiously arranged, and on the other side, her favourite spoon.

Whoops, he'd forgotten something—the doily.

He retrieved a white paper doily from a drawer beside the stove and positioned it under the bowl. In this way the bowl wouldn't slip, which was just the way she liked it.

That was it. Done. The breakfast of champions.

He popped the pan into the kitchen sink, where it joined a crowd of last night's dirties, and he clipped shut the little lid, on the little box, which was one of many little boxes in a new plastic tray. "MON AM" was empty.

Now there was time for Clifford to prepare himself.

Time for a quick smoke whilst he waited for the drugs to dissolve in the hot semi-skimmed milk. Time for a slurp of coffee-cum-treacle whilst the cornflakes went soggy, which was just the way she liked them.

Out in the backyard, Clifford enjoyed another slurp of his bitter black soup. He savoured the harsh tang of two heaped spoonfuls of unadulterated Nescafé, and with a wince of pleasure he sucked on his Embassy Number 1.

Breathe, deep breaths, and cough.

The Spider

Today the skies were cloudy. A herd of gray elephants floated by, right up there, above him, in the sky. It sounded like the start of a brand new song, and he'd write it later on.

Clifford didn't look too shabby for a forty-five-year-old man who eked out an unreliable living from giving private guitar lessons. Then again, the ex-rocker, and erstwhile fanny magnet, had worn a forty-year-old face for the best part of twenty-five years.

Oh shit! He noticed that his ciggie was three-quarters sucked and so, by this murky measure of time, the cornflakes had soaked long enough to render them acceptably soft.

Dropping his fag end into a flowerpot that had blossomed into an ashtray, Clifford looked down at his feet. They were the green-sneakered feet of a child stuck onto the legs of a fully-grown man: Clifford's twiggy legs, and Clifford's pathetic feet.

But now was not the time to worry about his unmanly feet.

It was time to go back inside. Time to say goodbye to the clouds and let them drift away to who-knows-where. Time, once again, to face those skittish arpeggios whose rise or fall seemed solely dependent upon whichever way the elephants were blown at any particular moment.

At times like these, Clifford's unmanly stomach never failed to churn.

2

Enter the most awkward butler in the world.

This was Clifford's normal impersonation during his main morning duty. He fumbled into the dingy front room with the tea tray, and the bowl, and the napkin, and the special spoon. The partial darkness did not impair his vision unduly, and in actual fact Clifford liked the gloom. He wore it like a protective cloak. It shielded him from harsh eyes, and harsh words, and harsh thoughts; or at least that's what he liked to think.

"There's a total eclipse today, Suzie," he said, as he negotiated his way towards the coffee table.

"Fuck off."

"No seriously, there is. That'll be fun to have a little look at, eh?"

"Fuck off."

"Well, I know you're not meant to look at it directly; that's people in general I mean, not you specifically." He put the tray down on the table. "It said on the radio that an eclipse can damage your eyesight if you stare right at it with your naked eyes. Perhaps we could take turns using your sunglasses…you know, the dark ones, or maybe get a piece of card with a pinhole in it and look at it on another piece of card, you know, projected on."

"Fuck off."

"OK, maybe it's only a partial eclipse."

"I mean just fuck off in general."

From many years of service, Clifford knew that this was a fairly mild reaction from his wife, in response to the delivery of her breakfast. Sometimes she said nothing at all, mesmerised by a section of vacant wall or a plain piece of black leather upholstery. But often he had known her to be extremely vocal. Wild screams for help, anguished prayers for relief, and tearful apologies, all of which were deluded. These were interleaved with venomous declarations of disgust or contempt for penis-wielding pigs who served up shit for breakfast; all of which were distressing. Accusations of neglect, or poisoning, or rape were common; all of them were false and simply the symptoms of the illness, or the medication, or a combination of both.

Squeezed into the front room was a black leather couch, which had seen better days, and its little brother, a comfy chair with patches on the arms that had been well worn to whiteness.

The threadbare carpet was on the verge of blackness. In its well-shagged youth, it might've been brown or orange, and precisely how it had descended into such a wretched state was a mystery—perhaps a lack of Shake n' Vac. Then again, after many colourful years, it could have simply given up and gradually absorbed the blackness from the rest of the room.

And of course, there was the rickety coffee table, IKEA's blackest, which was now supporting the tray, and the bowl, and the special spoon; oh, and don't forget the doily.

The Spider

Clifford groped his way over to the window, which was filled with memories of happier times in the well-lit world outside, and the curtains, which were neither open nor closed, he yanked open.

Suzie was curled into the comfy chair like a sloppy combination of Buddha and Morticia Addams. It was difficult to detect where the black leather started and Suzie ended. Even her pallid hands, poking out of her black sleeves, merged into the white patches. She screamed at the incoming of additional daylight.

"Stop it. Stop it. You're trying to kill me."

"No, I'm not," he sighed.

"Help!" she cried out to phantom rescuers. "He's going to rape me."

"Oh, Suzie, please."

"You won't get away with it, you filthy rapist."

To a background of whimpers from the chair, Clifford rubbed his stubbly chin, and as if a prayer was beginning to form, he cast his bloodshot eyes towards the ceiling. For a few moments, he studied the nasty cracks above. He followed their lightning patterns across the room, and he wondered how much more damage the plaster could withstand before the whole thing came crashing down on his head.

Eventually, he took a step towards his wife.

"Get away from me with your stinking penis."

Without a word, Clifford returned to the window and looked out at his small and unattractive front garden.

"It's not healthy skulking about in the shadows all day," he said, as he tried to calm his jangling nerves.

"Why don't you go outside and get some fresh air? The garden could do with a bit of tidying up, especially around the edges. Just for half an hour, eh? Get your mind off things."

"Fuck off."

By now, Clifford was happy to oblige, and with the luxury of fresh illumination, he scurried over to the door. It opened into a tiny hallway, which in turn led to the front door.

"Where are you going?"

"Out."

Suzie's anger suddenly flipped into pitiful timidity. "No, please Cliffy, don't go out, don't leave me," she whined.

"I've got to go out."

"Why?"

With his hand on the knob, he paused to pull another whopper from the excuses section of his mind. "I've got to post a letter."

"What letter?" As always, her period of pathos was extremely short-lived.

"It's an invoice."

"It's an invoice for what?" Suzie's paranoid suspicions were taking back control, and her tone had hardened once again.

"For a lesson I gave last week."

"Didn't you get paid at the time?"

"No."

"Why not? You always get paid at the end of the lesson."

The Spider

"Not always, and this time I forgot to ask." Clifford was a bad liar.

"You forgot! That's just typical of a man. You're all such fucking dickheads." Her rage ranted back into the room. "Oh, I forgot something as well. I forgot that you're a fucking moron."

It was a cruel assault, but maybe she was right. Only a moron would endure this torture day after day for as long as he had. Or perhaps it was cowardice, or apathy, or something much worse. All he knew was that he needed to get out for a brief respite before his brain disintegrated, because if it did he would be no use to anyone.

"I'm going out. Eat your breakfast."

He pushed open the door and disappeared into the hall. A few seconds later, Suzie heard the front door slam shut. She stared down at the tea tray, the bowl on the doily, the napkin, and the special spoon.

"Please don't leave me," she whispered to the essence of Clifford that was left hanging by the window.

3

Clifford sat on the back seat of the bus and contemplated his lack of letter.

Apart from the driver, and one old lady sitting near the front with her shopping trolley, he was alone. Upstairs might have been chock-a-block, but down here there was nobody in his space, which was just the way he liked it. Plenty of room to explore his seedy deceptions.

He hated lying. It was so demeaning. It wore away what little self-respect he had left, but what else could he do? The truth was even seedier, and he couldn't bring himself to consider it too closely, let alone confess to it. After all, he was a letter-less man, with tiny feet to boot.

He should focus on the mission. Yes, the mission: his shameful, clandestine, monthly mission to Golightly's, the newsagent, on the other side of town.

The bus juddered to the next stop, and the old lady, with her weekly groceries in tow, struggled off.

Out through the mud-spattered window next to his face, he could see a postman emptying the contents of a red letterbox into a gray sack. Clifford had nothing to give him; he never did. Nobody to write to for help; this was the curse of a letter-less man.

The bus jerked away, leaving the postman to his collections and driving Clifford towards recollections of a time when he was a different man, when he hadn't been as sensitive about the seedier side of life.

Twenty years before the back seat of the bus, Clifford had been gearing up for his one and only musical triumph; perhaps semi-triumph is more accurate.

In those days, just as now, he wore a craggy face, but in no way did it seem to hold him back. With a brand new plectrum and the eagerness of youth, he had strummed his way around most of the scabby nightspots up north, doing his best to flesh out from within the rugged persona created by his face. Was he talented? Who knows? He wasn't bad, and the more he strummed the more those sweaty six strings seemed to co-operate and play along with him.

In the beginning, you could have counted the band's fans on the fingers of one hand, but all that dismal obscurity was set to change with the launch of their latest song—a jangly anthem about love in the slums. Its punchy lyrics promised that better times were just around the corner for every disenchanted kid, and so this mediocre mantra captured the imagination of the hormonally rebellious youth of Britain. The song sold well, and soon the quirky quartet acquired a manager who was heavy in the gut but light in the head.

Shortly afterwards, during a bargain basement tour of students' unions, Clifford began to find himself swamped by adoring female attention. Horny girls of every size and colour, in a variety of shapes and without much clothing, appeared from nowhere and wanted to fuck him.

The Spider

"Cliff, Cliff, Cliff," they would scream from the front row during the gigs. And then after the gigs they would fuck him. Backstage or side-stage, at the stage door or up a nearby alleyway, Clifford had been well and truly fucked. Sometimes it was a threesome—with another little slut waiting for her turn—and often on the back seat of a clapped-out minibus with the driver watching intently, the sad old pervert.

Alas, those days were over.

There was no such rampant rumpy-pumpy on the back seat of his current rocky ride, and as the bus rumbled to a halt at another stop, Clifford struggled to remember the last time his pathetic penis had seen *any* real action. How unmanly!

It was London Road already, and the smooth white-marble domes of the Hindu temple caught Clifford's eye. Solid against the boisterous gray sky, this structure was a testament to ancient Vedic principles, and a well-known local landmark. In its grounds, he could see the stirrings of some sort of Indian celebration. People milled and chatted and laughed and kissed. It looked like there was going to be a wedding.

Golden silk kurtas, embellished with gemstones, chatted excitedly to a throng of rich burgundy sarees. Fertile crimson cholis, embroidered with elegant Zardozi motifs, danced with turquoise georgette lehngas. Purple touched cheeks with its cousin magenta, whilst floral and bandhani gowns gyrated with joy.

The vivid colours and euphoria were a marked contrast to Clifford's attire and demeanour, and as he studied this blissful show through the dirty glass window, he began to feel somewhat uneasy with his part as the lonely voyeur—the saddest role in the whole production.

One young woman, at the edge of the jubilant crowd, spotted Clifford's avid attention, and with a cheeky grin, she waved to him as he peered through the window. Lamely, like some hapless peeping tom, he waved back. What a tosser!

The girl's dusky skin, and the radiant yellow of her saree, reminded him of Suzie. Not the Suzie of today, but the saucy little sexpot Suzie on the night they had first met.

4

Suzie stabbed the earth with a pointy trowel. It was a nasty-looking tool that had turned rusty along the edges from years of unemployment.

She was kneeling in the front garden, on a patch of flattened grass, and wounded the ground half-heartedly. Her intention was to clear the soil borders and lay some bricks along the edge of the turf as part of a horticultural tidying exercise, but already she was bored after only six feet of restoration work.

Suzie's attention span was remarkably short. Fifteen minutes of anything, even the most interesting conversation or the most fascinating television show on the planet, was the maximum that her defective concentration could stand.

It wasn't always the case. Back in the days when she had first met Cliffy, before the addling of alcohol, the damage from years of daily dope, and the excess of powdery snortings, she had been able to focus for hours. Back then, she had been able to remember song lyrics, and friends' birthdays, and kind words.

Pleased with her progress, Suzie stood to inspect the hard work.

Dr. Cassidy, the silly old bugger, would have been proud.

"Impressive therapeutic endeavours; well done Susan," he would've said if he had been there to witness her toils.

Cliffy would've been proud as well.

She had made it out into the garden all on her own, and she had done something useful—not much, but useful all the same. With nothing more than a rusty trowel, a few red bricks, and her wits, she had completed an important bit of tidying up.

Triumphantly, Suzie threw back her head and looked up into the sky, but the sky turned out to be a disappointment. The dark clouds above reminded her of slugs—big gray slugs that slimed across an otherwise perfect sky.

Those slugs annoyed her. They spoiled a beautiful blue sky—the perfectly soft blue of a baby boy's romper suit.

Suzie huffed.

Those slugs brought Cliffy to mind. He slimed around and spoiled things. He fussed too much, and his fussing made her stressed and frustrated, and angry and sad. Nonetheless, she loved him; or at least she loved him for the odd fifteen minutes when she focussed on loving him. For the rest of the time…who knows.

Suzie knew that when she was mollycoddled into anger, her subsequent outbursts were often wicked. But Cliffy understood her, and he would never leave her. He needed her like she needed the little pink ones.

But Cliffy made her feel trapped, and she suspected that he enjoyed his controlling ways far too much

The Spider

and exercised his caring duties with a scary diligence. On many occasions Suzie was frightened, and her fear led to stress, which led to frustration and anger and sadness.

Now she noticed that the bricks she had just laid were ever so slightly cockeyed. The imperfection was stressful, and Suzie bent over to tap them into line with the trowel.

Plink…plink…plink.

These were bloody stupid bricks.

"Bastards," she spat, and the tapping intensified.

PLINK…PLINK…PLINK.

The bricks were proving to be uncooperative, resistant to correction.

"Fuckers!" she squalled and swung her arm again and again and again. Her fat breasts swayed, her bingo wings wobbled, and she began to sweat.

CLANG…CLANG…CLANG.

Out of breath, Suzie broke off the attack. She straightened up and sighed deeply several times. The bricks had offended her. They would have to be removed and rejected, replaced with nicer bricks that conformed nicely to Suzie's image of how the world should be.

Only now did she notice the sordid spectacle taking place in the neighbour's garden. Over the low wooden fence, Suzie could see Max, a loathsome mongrel, thick with Jack Russell genes, copulating with a garden gnome. The ornamental dwarf had long since lost his little fishing rod, which had broken off in one of Max's previous sexual attacks. Nevertheless, his inane grin, fixed in plaster, seemed to suggest that he was in some way enjoying Max's fervent thrusts from behind. Then again, it could've been a grimace, not a grin, and his chipped and faded thoughts could've been elsewhere—perhaps at the local fishing rod shop—whilst he waited patiently for Max to finish his business.

"Oh, for God's sake," Suzie exclaimed in disgust, "not again, you dirty little bastard. I know your game; you're doing it to spite me, aren't you!"

Max continued to thrust, and the gnome continued to think about rods.

"Filthy rapist," screamed Suzie, "stop it at once. I said stop it. Do you hear me! Stop shagging that gnome!"

Max didn't stop. He cocked his head in her direction and licked his steaming lips.

Incensed, Suzie bobbed down and ripped up two of the bricks that she had just laid down. These disobedient bricks might be of some use after all. She stood with a brick in each hand and gave Max another chance.

"I'm warning you!" she shouted, as she banged the bricks together. "Get away from that gnome, or else."

It was the point of no return for Max. There was no way he could stop now and stuck out his tongue to pant his way into climax.

Suzie flung the first brick. It was a pretty good throw—accurate but, alas, too powerful. The brick skimmed the top of the dog's head and landed by some unkempt privet. Tongue engorged and dribbling, Max seemed oblivious to the attack. However, Suzie had the

The Spider

measure of him. The practice throw had allowed her to make minor mental adjustments to her technique, and now she pulled back her arm to launch the decisive, skull-crushing shot. But she was disturbed.

"Mrs Williams?" In her eagerness to kill the canine rapist, Suzie had completely failed to notice a Ford Ka pull up to the kerb only twenty yards from her house. She hadn't seen the slim and sexy blonde-haired girl slide out of the car and strut up to the garden wall.

"Mrs Williams?"

Brick in hand, Suzie spun around to confront the visitor.

"Mrs Williams?" asked the new arrival for the third time. Her sweet smile, cheery disposition, and pert breasts were an instant irritation. "Are you Mrs Williams?"

"What do you want?" Suzie was in no mood for chitchat with this dolly bird.

"Hi, Mrs Williams, I'm Bev."

Suzie was stone-faced.

"Beverley Golightly. I'm from the Ga Ga Club."

Suzie dropped her brick.

5

It was 1985—the students' union at Swansea Polytechnic, and a jaded auditorium known locally, and inaptly, as the 'concert hall.' The breeze block and single glazing seemed incapable of holding any atmosphere, and any good news was sure to asphyxiate within moments of wandering in. This was a place that should have been incapable of harbouring any pleasant surprises for anyone.

Up on the stage, Clifford was strumming his guitar when he first set eyes on Suzie, and it was in that moment, with an unsuspecting glance in the wrong direction, that his lifeline veered onto a totally new and mysterious direction.

There on the front row, her radiant yellow mini-dress was clearly visible through the miasma of cigarette smoke and human perspiration. Her racy décolletage revealed a dusky cleavage that glistened salaciously with warm sweat. What a magnificent bosom! Clifford missed a chord change, but nobody noticed.

The girl's alluring doe eyes had irises so huge and brown that there was scarcely any room left over for the white bits to peep out from behind her long-lashed lids. Her eyes could've easily cast the most powerful enchantments with hardly a second blink.

She smiled at him with a calm and calculated coyness. If this was not enough to set his instrument on fire, she followed that smile with a slow and sexy wiggly-fingered wave; a wave meant for him—not for the lead singer or the bass player or the drummer or any combination of the four members. It was Clifford's wave, and his alone.

Strangely invigorated by the scrutiny of those fabulous eyes, Clifford hammered his guitar like a wild man.

Something was not right; something wonderfully awful was happening, and as the band began their best-known jangly ballad, the twang of his guitar was echoed by a twang within Clifford's head. Something had snapped in the mechanism of his mind, possibly a strut designed to support reason had broken, or maybe a gasket binding rationality to wisdom had blown.

Perhaps it was the effects of some maddening biochemicals that had been activated by a flux of weird particles recently emitted from the sun and which were now whizzing through his brain—a potent combination that never failed to help Cupid turn sensible fools into dribbling idiots.

Whatever it was, Clifford was smitten.

But no sooner had this exhilarating malady taken hold of him than the dreaded symptoms began to kick in.

As the band finished its final song of the evening, and with deafening cheers ringing in his ears, Clifford looked down at the spot where the doe-eyed girl had stood only moments before. He was hoping to beckon her to join him for a drink, but to his horror she was no

The Spider

longer there. He scanned the entire front row, but she had disappeared.

His stomach churned, his brain went into spasm, and he panicked. To protests from the band's roly-poly manager, he ditched the encore and dashed to the stage door.

He hurtled down a set of concrete steps and out into the side street, and there, like a wild man, he searched for the radiant yellow minidress, but it was nowhere to be seen.

He forced his way through a gang of boisterous groupies that had already started to form. Once he was spotted, there were cries of "It's Cliffy" and "Over here, Cliffy" and "Cliffy, give us a snog."

"Cliffy, sign me tits," screamed one teenage girl as she exposed a pair of chest pimples in his face.

"No, get away from me," he snarled, pushing past the almost-breasts, and the outstretched arms, and the puckered lips.

His staggering escape wobbled into a jog that quickly became a serious sprint down to the corner, and then right up to the main doors of the hall. There, in front of the steamy glass, he skidded to a stop and scrutinised the exodus of the encore-deprived fans that poured out onto the concrete plaza. Clifford was frantic for a flash of radiant yellow fabric among the swelling crowd. But there was none.

Why was he acting like a complete fool?

He could slither back down the side alley and have his wicked way with one of those eager beavers at the stage door, perhaps several, but for some intangible reason his heart wasn't in it anymore. Why was he so flustered about that one particular girl in the yellow dress?

He didn't believe in such ridiculous happenings as love at first sight. It was a laughable fallacy, up there with green cheese moons and Santa's sleigh. However, he was at that ignorant age when the rhythms of Mars were far more comprehensible than the melodies of heartsong.

After a restless night of pining in a flimsy bed-and-breakfast, Clifford spent most of the next day silently sulking. He had sulked on the back seat of the tour bus, all the way to Aberystwyth, where they were due to play their next gig. He had sulked whilst flicking through *The News of the World*. He had sulked into a bag of soggy chips and over a revolting pint of flat ale.

He didn't want to do the gig; in fact, he didn't want to touch his guitar again. But his bandmates were in no mood for a grumpy and unreliable Clifford, and after a hearty dollop of teasing and an exchange of harsh words, he was bullied into turning up for the sound check. If it went well, without any hitches or arguments or anything else that might piss him off, he might go on to play one last time at the gig…but with sulking reluctance.

Once the mixers had been set, and as the sounds of the rehearsal began to fade, Clifford turned to prop up his guitar in its chrome-plated stand, and that's when he saw her standing in the wings, to his right.

It took a few moments for Clifford's mind to acknowledge what he was seeing. The radiant yellow

The Spider

dress had gone and was replaced with a pair of skin-tight denim jeans, and now she wore a luminous green T-shirt that strained to contain her bosom. Yet, the ice-melting eyes, the lustrous black hair that fell to her waist, and the smile, which could whip any man's stomach into somersaults, were still the same.

Clifford could remember that his legs had turned to jelly, and he had to crouch down on the pretence of adjusting a strap or twiddling with a knob on his guitar before gaining his composure and walking over to her.

"You came back," his voice trembled as he stated the obvious.

"I'm Susan…Suzie, if you like," she enchanted with her melodic Welsh accent.

"Clifford."

"I know."

"How did you get in here?"

"I gave the bouncer a blow job," she said, giggling.

Clifford was gobsmacked. His face dropped, and he recoiled by a step.

"I'm only joking, silly," she said, noticing his distress. "I told him I was your sister, with an important message from home."

He was relieved.

"I don't fuck on a first date," Suzie warned after that gig in Aberystwyth. But she did on the second… and on the third, and five times on the fourth.

So began a stormy and passionate romance.

Suzie packed in her job at an undertaker's office in Brecon to become Clifford's permanent companion, and at the strict exclusion of all other women.

It turned out that Suzie was a talented singer, and despite the vexation of their manager, she would often perform backing vocals with the band.

This was a special time in Clifford and Suzie's life. They banged and clattered along the coastline of North Wales. They snorted and cavorted up through the Lakes and drank their way into Scotland. By the time the band returned to Manchester, where the tour had begun so many months before, they were both exhausted and ill, but there was good news waiting for the band.

It appeared that a well-known record label was keen to sign them up, and a meeting had already been arranged with some music industry executives from CBS to discuss a contract. Negotiations went well as far as their greedy and brainless manager was concerned, but it was shortly after the deal had been hashed out and rapidly signed that things started to go wrong.

It seemed that the drummer would receive the least money, whereas the lead singer would get the biggest slice of the financial pie, excluding the manager's secret remuneration package.

Suzie objected on Clifford's behalf, who, as she pointed out, wrote most, if not all, of their song melodies. The bass player said it was none of her business, and Suzie gave him a mouthful of abuse.

The lead singer insisted that the deal was a good one. He went on to make harsh accusations about Clifford's declining level of skill with the Stratocaster and his overall commitment to the band since he'd hooked up with Suzie.

The Spider

"Fuck you lot, I'm off," said the drummer, as he slammed the door and stormed away forever. He was no real loss, as drummers are ten a penny. The real end of the deal, and the band, came a few minutes later, when Suzie persuaded Clifford to walk, leaving the others to gawp at each other in disbelief.

Perhaps it was an ill-considered move. Employment was not that easy to find for a guitarist who had almost made it into the big time, but failed. Nevertheless, for several years Clifford managed to work as a session musician with other groups, mainly in some smoke-filled studio but occasionally at a concert. In addition, he began to teach guitar to a startling array of delusional would-be rock stars, and school children whose parents wanted to turn them into Mark Knopfler.

Slowly the session work dried up, although, until recently, he continued to bang out 'Bohemian Rhapsody' and other hits with a tribute band that occasionally required his services at various Queen Conventions. It was a sad day, only twelve months ago, when even this engagement came to an abrupt and unpleasant end following a nasty incident—an event that had enraged Suzie, who had always been a huge fan of Freddie Mercury.

Now only the tutoring brought in a meagre musical income.

***

It was a dutiful sleeping policeman, taken too quickly by the careless driver that jolted Clifford out of his reverie and back to the bus.

Whilst off in daydream land, he hadn't noticed that several more passengers had joined him for the ride. One was only a couple of seats away on the back row…the impudent bastard.

Clifford panicked. How long had he spent replaying the younger days of his life?

He snapped his head around and frantically studied the nondescript street that rolled past his window, trying to spot a familiar shopfront and gain his bearings, but it seemed that there were only unrecognisable chippies and bookies and Asian costermongers.

It was with a sudden relief that he saw the familiar semi-naked blonde-haired girl on the corner of the approaching junction. Her voluminous bosom, fettered with nothing more substantial than white lace, was the sign that he hadn't gone too far.

His stop was coming up, the next one on this route.

Clifford pressed the bell. It was almost time to get off.

6

Freddie Mercury was dead. He had been dead for twenty years.

"Remember Freddie!" said Bev Golightly—young, pretty, pert, and irritating.

Suzie was solid and silent, with a brick at her feet.

"The convention at Ainsdale," said Bev.

An immediate reaction wasn't forthcoming from Suzie.

"The special memorial convention," Bev explained.

Freddie Mercury: Somebody to Love.

The convention: The Show Must Go On.

Suzie grimaced as her rusty mental trowel struggled to dig up some recollection that would make sense of this encounter.

"Mrs Williams, I'm the new Events Officer for the Ga Ga Club," said Bev, with a self-important smile. "We talked on the phone last week."

Suzie scowled. She was feeling under pressure, but behind the image of a telephone, she unearthed a tiny memory of a conversation and dusted it off.

Bev's chesty grin faded, and the air turned uncomfortable. "You seemed very upset on the phone and said that you had to see me urgently, something about going to the convention this year. I was in the area, so I thought I'd pop in."

The penny dropped into the faulty mechanism that was Suzie's mind, and it switched on a whole new persona, intense but contrite.

"The convention, yes, I've got to go, I've got to go."

"OK, that's great. I love your enthusiasm."

"Please let me go; you've got to let me go."

"Of course I'll let you go," Bev said, puzzled. "Why wouldn't I?"

"Because of what happened last year."

"Why? What happened last year?"

Nobody at the Ga Ga Club had thought to tell Bev about what happened last year. Suzie's deluded misunderstanding had turned into an argument, which had turned into a scuffle and a lunge with a broken glass, and an ambulance rushing to join the convention.

"Oh, nothing really," Suzie back-pedalled when she realised that Bev had not been updated by the previous Events Officer, "just a little quarrel."

"You seem quite stressed up about it."

"Oh, no, not me, I always thought that the whole thing was blown out of proportion. I wanted a chance to explain to you, face-to-face, that there's nothing to worry about. I wanted to make sure that I was allowed to go again this year."

"Well, I can't see why not—"

"Oh, that's brilliant, thank you."

"…but then again I don't know anything about this quarrel—"

"I can assure you I'm a new woman, totally changed from last year."

The Spider

"…and perhaps I should check with the club's president." Bev reached into her fake Dolce & Gabbana satchel and retrieved a mobile phone.

"No, no," Suzie said, bouncing over to Bev like a giant black space hopper, "there's no need to bother him over such a stupid matter."

Bev was distracted from her dialling and paused between a six and a seven.

"Please come in for a cup of tea," Suzie said, gesturing to the house.

"That's a very kind offer, but I'm dead busy. I'm doing the rounds on a few other members of Ga Ga today, just saying hello and making sure everything's running smoothly for the convention. So if you're happy now, I've really got to get going."

"No, you fucking haven't," Suzie snapped, then instantly softened. "Please, I've got some lovely cake, and I need to talk to you about some other things."

"Well…" Bev pressed 'cancel' on her mobile.

"Come on, you'd love a hot cup of tea and a nice slice of parkin."

Bev returned the phone to her bag. Events Officers had to do an outstanding job, especially new ones. They had to schmooze with the membership, and they couldn't afford to disaffect anyone. "Oh, OK then, just a quick one."

"Thank you, thank you, thank you," Suzie gushed as she opened the garden gate and ushered Bev inside. "What a lovely girl you are!"

"I don't want to disturb you any more than I have already."

"Nonsense, it was only a silly bit of gardening," said Suzie as she picked up the rusty trowel on their way to the front door, "and anyway, this is a good opportunity to talk because he's not in."

"Who's not in?"

Suzie ignored the question. "And he won't be back for ages. So that gives us loads of time to eat some secret cake and have a girlie chat."

7

Clifford looked up at the advertising hoarding, and the tired poster of the model in the white lacy bra. For the past seven months or more, ever since his missions had swapped to this part of town, the blonde-haired girl looking down from the billboard had promoted cleavage-enhancing brassieres.

Clifford was always pleased to see her. She was his uplifting beacon, guiding him on his missions.

Yet, after all this exposure, her toothy grin was starting to look decidedly weather-beaten, and he was convinced that her hearty bosom had begun to droop, but not by much, and it was still well worth a butcher's in Clifford's book.

Despite his gratitude for her continued presence, he was surprised that she was still here after all this time. Each month he expected to see that she had been replaced by an advert for toilet tissue or yoghurt or the latest BMW. He had assumed that the world of advertising was a dynamic one, which would demand a higher turnover of posters.

It seemed she had been forgotten.

Clifford wasn't complaining about the apathy or incompetence of the agent in charge of the board, but perhaps her ongoing display was an oversight by some dopey advertising manager.

What saddened Clifford was that she was showing signs of neglect.

One day soon, without proper attention, the peeling would be complete, and the girl would blow away in the wind.

Clifford would have gladly given her all the necessary attention if he had been charged with making the repairs and had permission to erect some scaffolding.

From where he stood beneath the gargantuan chest, it was only a short walk down a side street to reach Golightly's—the newsagent shop.

It was an exciting walk, but also an uneasy one.

His eyes would twitch, his tummy would fidget, and his knees would weaken with every step closer to his final destination.

At the shop door, Clifford paused and squinted through the glass.

Most of the interior was taken up by a central island of shelves. He knew that one side was filled with biscuits, boiled sweets, and envelopes, whereas the other was home to an impressive array of greetings cards.

After a moment of eager observation, Clifford felt sure that the shop was devoid of any customers, which was just the way he liked it.

As he pushed his way in, the bell above the door dinged. It announced his arrival to the empty shop, but it wasn't quite as empty as he had thought. Only now inside did Clifford spot an elderly gentleman in a black suit—a priest, who was fingering a packet of fascinating fruit sweets. Their eyes met, and without a word ex-

The Spider

changed, the clergyman swiftly returned the sweets to the shelf before moving over to study a set of innocent envelopes.

Clifford beetled over to the wall-mounted rack of magazines and feigned interest in *Gardener's Monthly*, or was it *Wood Whittler's Weekly*?

The presence of the priest had irritated him.

Fuck off, Father. Just buy your sweets and fuck off.

With a sideways glance, Clifford could see that the counter at the far end of the shop was manned by the proprietor; a middle-aged bloke with a major moustache who Clifford had assumed was Mr. Golightly.

This was a bonus.

Thank God it wasn't the young blonde-haired girl who was so often on duty.

Today he wouldn't have to suffer the embarrassment of being served with her sickly sanctimonious smile and her cheeky "Enjoy!" as she handed over his change.

Clifford returned his attention to the rack of magazines before him. The top shelf was packed with a fantastic collection of overlapping pornographic literature.

There was the latest edition of *Razzle*. But he could also see a copy of this month's *Fiesta*. Both were among his favourites.

Whilst trying to decide which one to purchase, Clifford set about the first step of his well-practised procurement manoeuvre. He bent over and picked up a broadsheet—*The Guardian*—from the pile at his feet. Unfolded and balancing on his left forearm, the paper was now ready to receive its clandestine consignment.

The next step was tricky for a man of Clifford's stature. At five-foot-five, he was not equipped with enough height to make this easy. To reach his target, and tease *Razzle* from its slot, would require an awkward stretch, an unmanly stretch on tiptoes.

Regardless of the priestly presence, Clifford was ready for action and he was on the verge of raising his arm when the doorbell dinged.

In came a young mother and her boy.

Whilst she made straight for the counter, the kid, about seven, knelt down next to where Clifford stood and began to rummage through the comics.

A horrified Clifford pretended to read the back page of *The Guardian* and tried to act as nonchalant as possible.

"Twenty Richmond Superkings," said the mother to the moustache.

"Mum, I don't know which one I want," whined the kid, as he gazed at *Ben 10* in one hand and *Spiderman* in the other.

"Oh, my God, Jamie, just get a fucking move on," squawked the mother.

These wise words were music to Clifford's ears.

"Can I have two?"

"No, you fucking well can't."

The kid made a hasty choice and dashed to his mother's side.

"And that," she growled, as she slapped *Ben 10* onto the counter.

Clifford's eyes never left his newspaper as both the foul-mouthed mother and her indecisive offspring

The Spider

barged past him on the way out. With a ding, they were gone.

He took the opportunity to have a sly peek at the priest, who appeared to have returned to a contemplation of the confectionery.

Act now!

Clifford combined an urgent hop with an outstretched flick of the wrist into one fluid movement. *Razzle* was retrieved and tossed into the centre of *The Guardian*. It took less than a second for the naughty nurse on the front cover of his magazine to be engulfed by political scandals, stock market fluctuations, and football results.

At the counter, Clifford presented his innocuous bundle to Mr. Golightly.

"I'll take those, please."

The newsagent never looked up, and the mighty moustache never moved.

He vetted the bundle and placed it into a blue plastic bag, and handed it over to Clifford, with the remnants of a tenner.

The priest had plumped for chocolate buttons, and as Clifford dinged his way out into the side street, everything seemed good with the world.

8

Bev was perched on the edge of the couch. Opposite her, on the other side of the coffee table, Suzie was curled into the armchair and hugging herself. She was transfixed by the breakfast bowl, which remained on the doily, on the tray, where Clifford had left it for her.

The bowl was still full.

Next to it, the special spoon had been joined by the gardening trowel.

"I can't believe it's been twenty years," Suzie whimpered.

"I know," said Bev, "I was only a baby."

Suzie's jaw clenched and she flashed her visitor with indignant eyes. Bev's freshness made her sad, more so than remembering Freddie. She combed back her black straggling hair with her podgy fingers and continued to reminisce.

"I think I cried for a whole week after the news broke."

"Yeah, my mum was the same," Bev chirped.

"I must've used ten boxes of Kleenex." Suzie felt the need to compete.

"Even my dad cried," said Bev.

Suzie thought about Clifford. She couldn't recall him crying, only smiling at the radio when they played 'Another One Bites the Dust'—*the bastard.*

"All those filthy bastards in the world," Suzie growled. "Dirty perverts, and flashers, and rapists, and nudists—*they're* allowed to live. Why did he take Freddie?"

Bev didn't seem to be fazed by Suzie's outburst. No doubt she met loads of odd people in her dad's shop, and she had plenty of experience in the peculiar department, with all sorts of weird but pathetically amusing people.

"I don't know," she said, playing along. "Perhaps it was because he was special or a genius or something; they seem to get taken first. My Nana says it's because God wants them close to him."

"Yes, I can believe that's right." Suzie mulled over Freddie's genius status and hugged herself more tightly than before.

"White with one sugar, if that's OK." Cheek was Bev's forté.

"What?"

"I'll have that cup of tea when you're ready."

"Tea, yes, that's a good idea. But you're not having any sugar. We don't have any sugar in this house."

"OK."

"We've got sweeteners."

"I bet you have," Bev smirked.

"You want one or two?"

"No thanks, I'm sweet enough already," Bev quipped.

"What?" Suzie seemed confused.

"I don't like the taste of sweeteners," explained Bev.

The Spider

"Really," Suzie sneered as she emerged from the armchair and headed for the kitchen. "So then, you want a cup of tea?"

"With milk, please, if you've got milk."

"Yes, we've got milk, but you can't have any sugar because we don't have any sugar in this house."

In Suzie's absence, Bev took an opportunity to glance around the room.

The décor was drab to the point of sad.

Above an empty hearth, the hardwood mantelpiece was bare, save for a white porcelain angel with a chipped wing, which caught her eye. There was a mosaic of yellow cracks clearly visible across its little seraphic face and all down its immortal gown, and the godforsaken ornament looked like it had been glued back together on more than one occasion.

To a background of brewing noises and cussing coming from the kitchen, Bev noticed a large stereo system alongside the armchair. Resting on top of the enormous speakers were two framed photos. Curiosity got the better of her. She got up from the couch and went over to have a closer look.

One showed Freddie Mercury in action on stage. The image was blurred, as if it had been taken in a rush or by an unskilled photographer, but it was definitely Freddie.

The other appeared to be a young couple in a wedding day pose. Bev picked it up. The groom, with long hair and a goatee, was wearing a brown suit that was far too big for him—probably borrowed. The bride was Suzie, but she was barely recognisable—slim and lustrous. The photo must have been taken many years ago.

"What are you doing there?" Suzie had returned with two mugs of tea.

"I was just admiring your photos."

"Get away from there."

Bev replaced the photos, moved back to the couch, and sat down.

"It's a good one of Freddie."

Suzie plonked the tea down on the coffee table and eyed Bev with suspicion.

"Did you take it?" asked Bev.

"What?"

"That photo of Freddie."

"Yes, of course I did," said Suzie, as she crawled back into her armchair.

"Where was the concert?"

Suzie was struggling with this quiz. She gazed at the photo, but nothing came to mind. One of her cheeks started to twitch, and her eyes bulged with concentration.

"I don't remember."

A wave of uneasiness swept over Bev. "Well, anyway, you must've been on the front row to get that close to him," she said, nodding at the photo.

"Yes, I was. I was close to him." Suzie's cheek calmed down. "He was so special, so exciting, so erotic in the way he moved around on the stage." Her eyes returned to their natural socket sizes. "His voice was so powerful. He was a genius, you know. Someone told me once that he was a genius, and I can believe it."

The Spider

"I think Brian May is a real genius."

"Who is?" Suzie turned to face her young visitor.

"Brian May, you know, the lead guitarist."

"Yes, I know who Brian May is, what about him?"

"He's a real genius."

Suzie was appalled. "Why would you say such a thing?"

"Well, because he's like a professor or something."

"No, he's not."

"Yeah, he is. He's an astronomer or something. He was on the TV the other night banging on about an eclipse that's happening sometime this week."

"Someone told me about an eclipse."

"He's coming this year."

"What?" Suzie was getting confused, and confusion led to stress.

"Brian May, he's coming to Ainsdale this year, with it being a special year—'Remember Freddie.' I'll probably get to meet him."

"Silly cow, why would he want to meet with you?"

"Because I'm the new Events Officer for Ga Ga, and I've been doing all the organising of things."

Bev picked up her mug and took a self-satisfied slurp. "No cake?" she enquired with a smile.

"None left," Suzie lied. "Cliffy must've eaten it all, the greedy bastard."

Bev laughed. Suzie didn't.

"Cliffy, is that your husband?"

"Yes."

"Is he at work?"

"No, he's gone to post a letter," Suzie huffed, "but he should be back soon."

9

For the whole of his bus journey home, Clifford had stood up near the driver's cubicle and held on to a pole for support.

The Guardian had been ditched in a bin shortly after leaving Golightly's, but the magazine was causing him problems. It was stuffed into the waistband of his jeans and covered over by his Moody Blues T-shirt. With a bit of downward drift, the magazine was now in a most uncomfortable position, and it made sitting impossible. He needed to adjust its orientation, but he feared that the necessary manipulations might draw the attention of other passengers to his predicament.

He suffered in silence. The pain would be worth it in the end.

At the stop nearest his house, Clifford hobbled off. Alighting this close to home did not comply with his routine mission plans, and it made him nervous. He didn't want anyone he knew to spot him getting off the bus. News of the bus ride might get back to Suzie and trigger a "why were you on the bus?" inquisition, which would inevitably lead to a nasty paranoid rant. But the *Razzle* down his jeans was misbehaving, and the discomfort it was causing outweighed his worries about public transport. Better to run the risk of being rumbled for the bus than to walk any more than he had to.

Royston Cole

As he turned into his home road, the chafing down below became unbearable, and Clifford had to stop. To continue any farther without a critical re-jigging of the clandestine literature might lead to serious manhood damage, or at least that's how it felt.

Less than twenty yards away, Mr. Warner from No. 6 was washing muddy football imprints from the bonnet of his precious Morris Minor—again.

Within striking distance of Mr. Warner, four small hooligans, out of school with a bad case of truancy, were playing a loud game of football. Their mothers were busy gossiping over front garden fences. Every so often, one of these ladies tore herself away from debating the adulterous scandal at No. 42 to suggest to the unruly kids, in a stream of expletives, that they should take their football and their truancy to the local park.

Mr. Warner grumbled and tutted as he listened and washed, the miserable bastard.

From farther up the road came a whistling postman who was happy with his heavy sack, the cheerful bastard.

Clifford was disinclined to manipulate the magazine in plain sight of all these bastards, who would instantly turn into ardent observers the moment he reached for his packet.

His only hope was an alleyway to his left, and shuffling sideways into the shadows, he leant against a wall behind a purple wheelie bin.

It wouldn't take long to carry out the corrective procedure, but best it was done in private. Once his T-shirt was lifted, he tugged on the *Razzle* and succeeded

The Spider

in raising it up by a couple of inches. Then, through his jeans, he coaxed the bottom section along to the right by the same amount. With his T-shirt down, Clifford pumped his legs and performed a few pelvic thrusts to check on his mobility. All was fine, and the relief was blissful.

With a newfound spring in his step, Clifford burst back onto the road and straight into the path of big busty Barbara, his next-door neighbour.

"Jesus Christ, Cliffy," she wailed, "I thought you were a mugger."

Mr. Warner looked up from his bonnet, and the gossips fell silent as they caught the whiff of fresh misconduct in the air. But the boys and their ball couldn't give a toss, and after a moment's pause in washing and tittle-tattling, neither could the others.

"Sorry," said Clifford.

"You're a naughty man, jumping out on innocent girls like that."

Barbara was a voluptuous middle-aged beauty who was far from innocent, or a girl. Clifford liked to watch her undulations from a distance, but up close she made him nervous with her flirtatious ways.

"What were you doing down there?"

"It's a shortcut," he stammered.

"From where?"

"From town."

"You little devil," she teased, "sneaking into town without Suzie."

Clifford shrugged and tried to look innocent.

Barbara winked. "Next you'll be running off to Benidorm with a mistress."

"No, I will not," said Clifford, indignantly.

"What a pity! But you can't blame a girl for trying. Anyway, come on, whilst you're here you can help me carry these groceries." She handed him her heaviest Tesco bag.

They set off up the road, and Clifford was careful to be well out of the range of Barbara's free hand, which could easily turn to buttock pinching or crotch groping.

"How's Suzie doing? I've heard her shouting a few times, you know, through the wall."

"She's fantastic," said Clifford.

"Oh, that's good. I was a bit worried on a couple of occasions last week, but I suppose it's a woman's normal work to shout at her man."

At Barbara's garden gate, they both clapped eyes on Max, who was up against the handle of a watering can and thrusting his hindquarters.

"Bloody dog," said Barbara, "always shagging something. He's done my leg a few times, and leaves a shocking mess on my stockings."

Clifford looked down at her chubby calves, but he couldn't see any signs of trauma or canine residue.

"Anyway, I'd better go inside and get the old man's dinner on. His shift finishes in half an hour. Don't forget that if you need anything, you know where I am."

Clifford handed back her bag and watched as she waddled indoors.

As he pushed open his own gate and stepped onto the path, his unmanly stomach began to churn.

The Spider

He was hoping that Suzie was taking one of her little naps, and that he could slip in and straight upstairs without rousing her.

At the front door, whilst retrieving the key from his jacket pocket, Clifford glanced back at Max and the watering can. He couldn't help but smile as he remembered times gone by.

10

The tea was like tar, as if the essence of the infusion had been extracted with unbalanced zeal by squeezing the helpless teabag to within a millimetre of bursting point.

Bev regretted prompting Suzie for the tea. The dark terracotta brew, which would have been foul even with sugar, left a nasty taste in her mouth, and she shivered.

"Well then," Bev trilled into the silence, "whilst I'm here I might as well confirm a few details." From inside her bag she produced a notebook and a biro.

In the armchair, Suzie tensed up.

She was wary of people who wielded pencils and pens. Those sorts of people with notebooks and forms made her suspicious as they flicked through notes and made unpleasant decisions based upon their secret jottings.

Bev flicked through to a page that was already half-filled with scribbles.

"So, I guess it's two of you for the convention this year. Is that correct?"

"Me and Cliffy, yes, of course it is. Why would I go on my own?" Suzie shifted onto her other buttock.

"Well, you know, sometimes partners can't go, or won't go, with their other halves. You'd be surprised how many people go alone and perhaps meet up with friends when they get there."

Suzie didn't have any friends. "I don't want to go on my own."

"Good, so that's two seats on the coach."

"I can't go on my own."

"Now then," Bev continued, ignoring Suzie's distress, "this year the coach leaves from the main bus station behind the library in town."

"I can't go on my own."

"From Stand F, you got that?"

Suzie didn't seem to be listening.

"That's Stand F, Mrs Williams." Bev put down her pen and clicked her fingers for attention, "Stand F for Freddie; you should be able to remember that."

"I need Cliffy to go with me." Suzie was getting anxious.

"Yes, and I'm sure he will, but I've got to tell you that the coach will be leaving at nine o'clock sharp on that Friday morning. We won't be hanging around for any stragglers, so be there at least fifteen minutes beforehand to load your luggage. If you're late, we won't wait."

"We won't be late. We'll be there. Both of us will be there because my Cliffy loves me."

"Good."

Suzie rubbed her hands into the faded arms of her comfy chair. A tiny bit more black patent leather was worn away around the edges of the white patches.

The Spider

"He loves me," she chanted, and rubbed. "He loves me." She rubbed some more, turning darkness into lightness. "He loves me."

"I've no doubt."

Bev picked up her pen and began scribbling in the dreaded notebook. At one point she paused to look up at the cracked ceiling and mumble to herself.

Suzie stopped rubbing, and she followed Bev's preoccupied gaze as it wandered from the ceiling to the angel to the photos on top of the stereo.

Tapping the top of her pen on the tip of her tongue, Bev frowned and mumbled some more. She seemed to be struggling with a difficult puzzle, or perhaps she was trying to complete a complicated piece of mental arithmetic.

Suzie watched and waited and stiffened. Something wasn't right. An unpleasant decision was brewing.

Nodding at the solution to whatever problem had vexed her for the last two minutes, Bev seemed satisfied, and she returned to her notebook. Another couple of lines were terminated with a theatrical full stop. For now the important scribbling was over, and she looked up to find that she had Suzie's rigid attention.

"Right then," Bev said, forcing a smile.

They always forced a smile just before the unpleasantness was revealed.

"In terms of accommodation," Bev continued, "I guess it's a chalet for two."

"Yes, and I need the same chalet as last year," Suzie ejaculated.

"Do you really?"

"Yes, I do. Exactly the same one as last year."

"And why's that?"

"Two bedrooms, that's why." Suzie nodded to emphasize the requirement.

Bev was mystified. "Forgive my stupidity, Mrs Williams, but Cliffy is your husband, isn't he?"

"Yes."

"OK."

"And he loves me."

"Yeah, I've got that, but what's the problem?"

"I haven't got a problem."

"So, why do you need two bedrooms?"

"I need that chalet."

"Mrs Williams, I'm a single girl, so maybe I'm not an authority on these things." Sarcasm was not Bev's forté. "But don't husbands and wives sleep together, like in the same bed?"

"Don't argue with me; just put us down for that same chalet. I need one with two bedrooms."

"Well look," said Bev with a hint of irritation in her voice, "I don't know if I can guarantee a chalet with two bedrooms for a married couple."

Suzie was mortified. "You must."

"I must nothing," Bev announced, her eyebrows raised and her tone turning frosty. "It's a big event this year. We've got families coming from all over the UK, families with children who need those chalets with two bedrooms. So without some extenuating circumstances, I can't guarantee anything. What possible reason can you give me to justify two bedrooms?"

The Spider

"It's Cliffy, he's got the problem."

Bev cocked her head and waited for more information that wasn't forthcoming. "What sort of problem?" she prompted.

"He snores."

"He snores!" Bev was gobsmacked. "That's it?"

"It's very bad snoring."

"I don't doubt it, but that's not a valid reason. Hey, I'm no expert, but I think you'd find that most women have husbands who snore badly. That's why God invented elbows." She simulated a rib-digging manoeuvre with the elbow that was connected to the hand that held the pen.

"I don't know about any other husbands, only Cliffy."

"I'm sorry, Mrs Williams."

"You don't understand." Suzie's face was flushed. "I can't get any sleep."

"I'm sorry, Mrs Williams, you'll just have to invest in some earplugs."

Another secret note was about to be made, but Suzie wasn't finished.

"No, wait, it's his waterworks as well," she blurted. It was a lie, full of fluster and bursting with shame, sired by desperation and addled thinking. Clifford's urinary system was in perfect condition.

Bev's head snapped up from the paper and pen. "His what?"

"His waterworks…you know."

"You mean his—"

"Yes, his pisspot plumbing." Suzie pointed at the notebook. "So put that in your pad."

Bev was agog and turning ruddy with suppressed devilment.

"Wow, what a lucky lady you are! Not only does Mr. Williams snore like Vesuvius by all accounts, but he also wets the bed." Bev tried to hide her glee, but alas a little snigger slipped out.

"No, it's not like that. He just goes a lot."

"He does what?" Bev inquired.

"He goes a lot, especially during the night. Up and down he goes, up and down and up and down all fucking night. I don't get any rest. I wake up knackered and cranky. That's my problem, and that's why I need a chalet with two bedrooms."

"Yes, I can see you've got a problem." Bev moaned to control the urge to laugh out loud and calmed her trembling chest before she continued. "But I'm still not sure I can reserve you a special chalet with two bedrooms."

"Are you taking the piss?"

An insensitive tear broke free from Bev's mischievous eye and chuckled down her cheek before merrily diving on to the notebook. "No, of course I'm not."

A thought popped into Suzie's head. "It's his prostate."

"His prostate!" Bev was enjoying this development.

"Yes, it's his prostate. Did you know that lately he's been spending more and more time in the toilet?"

Bev shook her head, and Suzie went on.

The Spider

"Off he goes, every five minutes, and locks himself in the toilet for ages. An hour once; I was bloody bursting."

"Very strange, but as I said—"

Suzie interrupted as another thought popped into her head. "It could be the menopause."

"The menopause!"

"Male ones," Suzie declared adamantly. "They do exist. I saw it in a magazine at the hospital last week… or was it the week before."

"I'm not sure about that."

"Yes, it said that they can start as young as fifty."

"And how old is Mr. Williams?"

"Erhm…forty-five, I think."

"Look, Mrs Williams, your husband's bladder disorder is very unfortunate." Bev's voice wobbled, and she paused to regain her composure. "But, with respect, it's nothing special, and this year I think you're going to have to settle for one bedroom and one double bed."

"Do you want me to beg?"

"No, I don't want you to beg."

"Your sort, you always want me to beg."

"I'm just stating the facts."

"Shush," Suzie ordered, cocking her head towards the door. "Did you hear that?"

"I didn't hear anything."

"Shush, I said shush; are you deaf?" She put a podgy finger to her lips and listened intently. "I think it might be my Cliffy. He's back."

Suzie disengaged from the blackness of the armchair and heaved her bulk to a standing position.

"When he comes in here," she warned, glaring at Bev, "don't mention the chalets."

11

Despite Clifford's best efforts, the latch made an uncooperative click as he closed the front door. In the hallway, he held his breath. Was that Suzie's voice he heard coming from the living room? Probably not; it was just his imagination playing tricks, as all was now quiet. She would be in one of her medicated snoozes, flaked out in the armchair, snoring and muttering unconscious obscenities at dreamed-up rapists.

As always, his aim was to make it unnoticed to the first floor bathroom where he could stash his magazine behind the boiler.

This appliance was also the home of a big fat spider, black and hairy. In addition to her other conditions, Suzie suffered from arachnophobia, which made the boiler a perfect Suzie-proof hiding place for his naughty literature.

Clifford hadn't seen the spider for weeks, and he wondered whether it was still there in its dark, damp crevice by the hot water pipe. It might have moved out to another nearby house with juicier flies. Nevertheless, Clifford maintained a decent level of security by frequently reporting to a horrified Suzie with fictitious sightings of the hairy monster as it emerged for eight-legged walks along the shelf next to the toilet.

The need for magazines, in fact the whole comic affair, could have been avoided if he'd been able to use the computer. He'd heard that the web was born for porn, among other less satisfying applications. But it was Suzie's computer, in Suzie's bedroom, and she protected it with ferocious zeal and a secret password that was written on a Post-it note under the keyboard.

Even if he could log on, Clifford wasn't too clever with modern information technology, and he feared that he would be unable to cover his Internet tracks. On many occasions, he had considered buying his own computer, but he knew that laptops were very expensive, and in his Luddite opinion, you couldn't beat a good magazine, the outright ownership of it, the feel of it, the cheapness of it.

He took a careful step towards the bottom of the staircase, but his green sneaker found a faulty floorboard, which creaked like a traitor to the pornographic cause. Clifford froze, as if the floorboard were a landmine. He cursed his tiny feet for letting him down. What now? Should he give up on stealth and just make a dash for it? Even if the creak had woken Suzie, he could be at the top of the stairs, and almost to safety, before she struggled up from her chair and came out into the hallway to investigate the creak. A successful outcome to his secret mission might still be possible if he were quick.

But before he could take another step, and make another creak, the living room door opened, and Suzie emerged between Clifford and the stairs. She closed the door and swung around to confront him.

The Spider

"Did you get lost on the way home?" she growled. "No, don't tell me, you couldn't get stamps anywhere and had to deliver the letter yourself."

"You know that sarcasm is a good sign."

"Is a good sign of what?"

"That the new medicine from the hospital is working, and you're getting back to your normal witty self."

A cautious Clifford edged toward his wife and the stairs. With the porno package in his pants, he could not afford to have a fight or invite any form of physical contact with her.

"Fuck off."

"OK, whatever you want. I'm happy to fuck off upstairs and out of your way if you would let me get past."

He tried to ease his body through the obstruction, in between Suzie and the wall-mounted shelf, where the telephone sat but never rang.

She shoved him away, and the sudden jolt backwards dislodged the magazine. After an alarming drop, its bottom now rested precariously in the scrotal pouch of his underpants.

"For fuck's sake, Suzie, don't start this."

"Where've you been? You've been gone for ages."

"No, I haven't."

"Yes, you have."

"And you need a hobby apart from clock watching." Clifford was angry.

Suzie studied him with the keen eyes of a skilled neurotic. It was a quick yet thorough visual inspection from craggy face to unmanly feet. Clifford knew what she was doing. This was the paranoid examination that he had to endure whenever he came back from anywhere—even the backyard. He always felt violated by the scrutiny.

"What's wrong with your leg?" she asked.

"What, nothing."

"So why are you limping?"

"I'm not limping."

"Yes, you are."

"Well, if I am, it's probably just a bit of stiffness, in my knee, from the walk."

"You look like you've shit yourself."

"That's charming. You always have a way with words."

"Just shut the fuck up. We've got a visitor." Suzie raised a finger to her lips and nodded at the living room door.

A visitor was a rare event, and Clifford was intrigued. "Who is it?"

"Her name's Bev."

"And what does she want?"

A gap opened up beside the telephone shelf. Clifford sashayed through and made it onto the first step of the stairs. His desire to hide, or peruse, the magazine outweighed his intrigue.

"She's from the Ga Ga Club."

Clifford froze on the second step of the stairs. "The Ga Ga Club?"

"Yes."

When he turned around, his face was flushed with dread.

"What does she want?" he asked, suspiciously.

The Spider

"She's the new Events Officer."

"Did you invite her to come?"

"Maybe, but she's a personal friend of Brian May."

"This better not be about the—"

"Now hang on, Cliffy, don't get angry," Suzie interrupted.

"Oh, Jesus, I thought we'd agreed about this."

"No, I've agreed to nothing. It's you who's been agreeing with yourself."

"I'm not going to the convention. I've made that clear for ages."

Contriteness settled on Suzie again. She wrung her hands and tried to use the power of her doe eyes.

"Please, Cliffy, it means a lot to me, especially this year."

Clifford's demeanour hardened. He tried to resist the influence of her big brown eyes and her trembling bottom lip.

"No way, I'm not going again. I've told you this hundreds of times already."

"Please, Cliffy, it's been twenty years. It's 'Remember Freddie' this year."

"Suzie, I don't care anymore."

"Please, please, please." She bobbed up and down like an excited schoolgirl asking for permission to go to a party with the older boys.

"No, not after last year's fiasco; I don't think it's a good idea. Shit, are we even allowed to go again?"

Suzie flipped back to she-devil. "Last year, last year; I don't give a fuck about last year. That bitch asked for it."

"Oh, she asked for it, did she?"

"Yes, she did. You were there; you know what she did."

"'I'll have a broken glass in my bosom'—is that what she said?"

"Shut up, I don't want to think about it."

"'Ten stitches in my tits'—is that what she asked for?"

"Stop it."

"That poor girl; we just had a little chat at the bar."

"And she winked at you."

"Oh, yeah, sorry, the wink, how could I forget about the wink? An innocent friendly wink, but you went berserk, and you nearly went down for assault."

"You're being cruel."

"No, I'm not. I'm trying to look after you."

"You never look after me, not properly."

Clifford was dented by this jibe. "You ungrateful cow; I don't know why I bother sometimes. I must be mad."

"You're a bastard."

"No, Suzie, I'm not. So why don't you go back there," he said, pointing at the living room door, *"and get rid of your new friend."*

"She's not my friend. She's the Events Officer for Ga Ga."

"Yeah, OK, whatever—but get rid of her."

"I'll go on my own."

"What?"

"To the convention; I'll go on my own."

The Spider

"No, Suzie, you can't do that. What would Dr Cassidy say?"

"He said that everything should be as normal as possible, for me to get better."

This was true.

Dr Cassidy was the indifferent psychotherapist who left the golf course once a week to offer words of wisdom to people like Suzie and Clifford. He was convinced that Suzie's recovery would benefit from a happy routine that was full of normality—whatever that was.

"Suzie, my love, going to this convention is not going to help."

"Dr Cassidy said that I should have delicious days."

This was also true.

If Dr Cassidy had been able, he would have written out a prescription for 'fifty days of sheer delight.'

"Cliffy, the convention will be delicious."

"Maybe, but you know what you're like around other people. It could so easily go so wrong. I'm just worried about you. I don't know what I would do if there was any more trouble."

"Do you want me to beg, Cliffy?" Suzie whimpered. "I'll beg if you want."

The big doe eyes came into play yet again, and Clifford was unable to resist the enchanting power they had over him. His love for his wife might've been battered, but it was far from dead. His shoulders slumped. His heart was breaking. He didn't know what to do for the best.

"No Suzie, I don't want you to beg."

12

It was a big black cloud.
A massive bull elephant of a cloud, rogue and angry, rejected by the main herd that had passed over hours before.

It settled for a rest above Clifford's terrace. It blocked out the sunlight, much like an eclipse might do.

The whole street became dark.

The living room was plunged into gloom once again. It was as if Clifford's illuminating work at breakfast time had been undone by some mysterious force that had pulled the curtains shut again; but no, they remained open.

Bev was trying to write more notes in her little hardback book when Suzie bounded back in and flopped onto her chair.

Suzie didn't seem to notice the sinister scribbling, but the chair might have moaned with the stress of such extreme depression.

Suzie grinned. It was her first smile for months—an unnerving sight.

"This is my husband, Cliffy."

Clifford stepped down from the stairs and into the open doorway, where he hesitated.

"Cliffy, come in and meet our guest."

Clifford didn't want to go in and meet anyone.

"Cliffy, come in here."

Clifford stood at the edge of the gloom, uncomfortable and unnerved.

"Cliffy," Suzie growled, the grin disappearing, "please get your fucking arse in here now."

With a feeble sigh of resignation, and an indignant shake of his head, Clifford did what he was told and stepped into the battle zone. It occurred to him that it wasn't going to be easy to let Suzie down as tenderly as possible, eject the visitor as diplomatically as possible, and retreat to safety with his magazine and his sanity intact. But the sooner it was over, the better for all concerned.

"That's better. Now Cliffy, this is…oh…I've forgotten your name."

"It's Bev," their guest said, as she turned to meet the newly arrived alpha male.

"Hello," said Clifford.

He held out his shaking hand through the partial darkness, and as his eyes adapted to the dark, he focussed on the visitor's face. *Oh my God*, thought Clifford. It was the girl from the newsagent's; the girl from Golightly's; the Golightly girl who regularly processed his pornography through the till.

Bev squinted and blinked, and twisted on the couch to get a better look at the master of the household. She'd seen him somewhere before. Where was it? Was it in the pub? At the sports club? Was he a customer in her father's shop? Yes, he was. Oh yes, now she recognised him and remembered what he purchased from her.

The Spider

"Hello again," Bev said, her mouth curling into a wry smile. She did not shake his hand.

Clifford glanced nervously at Suzie.

Suzie was surprised.

"Hello *again*?" Suzie said. "Do you two know each other already then?"

"No," said Clifford, with the quickness of a bad liar.

"Yes, we do," corrected Bev. "Your husband comes in my dad's shop for his—"

"Newspaper," Clifford interrupted. His mind was racing as he tried to think on his unmanly feet.

"Which shop?" Suzie was confused.

"Golighty's," said Bev, "the newsagent on Hardman Street."

Suzie took her time and, with a pained expression, gave the location of Hardman Street some thought.

"Hardman Street—the one off London Road?"

"Yes."

"The one that's next to the municipal library?"

"Yeah, that's the one."

"But that's bloody miles away."

"Yes, it's the other side of town." Bev was in heaven. Here was a dirty old man and his fat loony wife; this was a piss-taker's dream. "Mr Williams is a faithful customer, always popping in and out."

Suzie's eyes bulged with the pressure of mixed-up thoughts behind them.

"Why do you go all the way over there when there's a paper shop on the next street?" she asked her husband.

"I think that Miss Golightly has got me confused with someone else," Clifford squirmed.

"No," said a grinning Bev, "I don't think so…Cliffy."

"Yes, in a busy shop like yours, with lots of people coming and going, it must be easy to get confused."

"Maybe, but I never forget a regular, or what they usually buy." Bev gave Clifford an impish wink, and he cringed.

"You're a regular?" Suzie was perplexed and getting agitated.

"No, not a regular," said Clifford.

"Then what—what's going on? What are you saying?"

Clifford didn't know what he was trying to say. Showing the spectacular traits of a terrible liar, he hemmed and hawed and shifted from one unmanly foot to the other.

"Well, come to think of it, Golighty's newsagent's shop—yes, I might've popped in once or twice whilst passing."

"Passing? Passing from where?" Suzie was not impressed. "It's the other side of bloody town."

"From lessons, when I was giving some lessons in Ribbleton."

"I didn't know you were giving lessons in Ribbleton." Clifford shrugged.

"For fuck's sake, Cliffy, sit down! You're making me nervous standing there."

Clifford wasn't sure he could sit down with the rigid magazine stuffed into his underpants. "I'd rather stand."

The Spider

"Sit down!"

As he lowered himself on to the arm of the couch, the strain on the magazine became too much, and with an audible crack, it folded in half. At the crease, a sharp edge dug into the flesh at the base of his penis. The sudden pain almost made him yelp.

"Who were you teaching in Ribbleton?"

"Oh, Christ, I don't know. A spotty student, some sweaty knobhead; I really can't remember. What does it matter? I don't tell you about every single detail of my fucking shitty existence."

"That's right, Mrs Williams," Bev chipped in, "all men have their little secrets."

"It's not a secret. It was a lesson. I had to walk down Hardman Street to get to the station. What's the big deal?"

"The station. You mean you went on the bus?" Suzie was mortified.

Clifford had blabbed his way in to the big deal, and he knew it.

"Oh, Cliffy," Suzie said, her voice wavering but wobbling on, "you went on the bus without me?"

"Yes." He couldn't look into her eyes, those wonderful eyes that were now wide with incredulity. He knew what he had admitted to, and shame forced his eyes away from hers. All that they could find were the cereal bowl, and the garden trowel, and the hopeless, dirty carpet.

She managed to swallow the hard lump of anguish in her throat. "But the bus," she whimpered as the tears formed. "I love going on the bus."

"Yes, I know." The treachery of it hit him in the chest.

"Why, Cliffy? Why did you go on the bus without me?"

"I was going to give a lesson."

"I could've come with you."

"No, you couldn't."

"Yes, I could. I could've sat in the corner or waited outside, at the bus stop, for you to finish."

"Suzie, you know you couldn't do that. Please try to understand."

"I love that bus."

"I know you do."

"You went on the bus without me."

"I know, and I'm really sorry."

"Was it the yellow one?"

"No, Suzie, it wasn't the yellow one. It was a green one."

She fought with her thoughts. Reds and blues and greens, but it wasn't the yellow one, not her special yellow one; and maybe that wasn't so bad.

13

There's nothing better than a good domestic. It's quality viewing.

But Bev was now at a loss. The Williams's domestic seemed to have stalled. As she studied them, both appeared to be frozen in time. Clifford stared at the floor, whereas Suzie stared at the photos on the stereo system.

Bev needed to inject a stimulant.

"Ahem. What about the convention—Remember Freddie?" she said.

Clifford stirred. "I'm not sure what my wife's already told you, but we're not sure yet if we can make it this year. So for the moment, just put us down as a couple of maybes." He pointed at her notepad.

"Definites," said Suzie, moving once more.

"Definite maybes," corrected Clifford.

"Definite definites." Suzie wasn't giving in.

"Definite definites?" said Bev. "Are you sure?"

"Definitely," said Suzie, winking at Bev and nodding at the notepad, "just the same as last year."

"Oh, Christ." Clifford's head drooped.

"Ignore him," Suzie said with disdain, "he's an E.L.O. fan."

"No way! My dad loves them, too," said Bev. "In fact, I'm named after the drummer."

Suzie wasn't impressed. "Really, I bet he's coming to the convention this year as well, with that fucking Brian May genius."

"'Sweet Talkin' Woman,' eh Cliffy." Bev was having fun again.

"Whatever." He wasn't in the mood.

"What? Who is? What sort of woman?" Suzie was filling up with paranoia.

"But it looks like one definite," Clifford said, pointing to Suzie, "and one maybe. Is that clear?"

"Look," said Bev, with faux contriteness, "if I'm going to cause an argument, then perhaps I should be leaving now."

"No, you stop where you are," Suzie barked at Bev, and then defiantly to her husband, she snarled, "Have you forgotten our little chat in the hall?"

Clifford was staring at the dirty carpet once again. He felt more entrapped than ever before.

"Hey, guys, before I go, all I can say is that this year's convention is going to be coola-boola, and you'd be fools to miss out," chirped Bev.

"Coola-boola! What the hell is coola-boola?" Clifford was appalled. He looked up in horror. In all his years of writing shitty lyrics, even at his worst, he had never stooped so low as to make use of such a terrible rhyming compound as 'coola-boola.'

"Yeah, you know, awesomatious," Bev giggled, "with film crews and celebs everywhere. I'll probably get interviewed for the TV, with me being the event organiser."

The Spider

"That'll be lovely for you," Clifford sneered. "Very awesome...atious! But as I say—"

"Hey," Bev said, ignoring his sarcasm and interrupting, "if you're really lucky, I'll introduce you to Brian May."

"Is Brian May going to be there?" Suzie was confused but enthused. "Wow, we can't miss that. Be honest, Cliffy, you'd love to go."

"Yes, Cliffy, stop playing hard to get. I bet you'd love to come." Bev gave him a knowing wink. "And Mrs Williams is keen."

"Deadly," squealed Suzie.

"Oh, I know; dear God, don't I know it." Clifford was struggling with the bombardment of babble and the pain in his penis.

"I've told you, Cliffy. I told you out in the hall. I'll go on my own if I have to. I will; and what will you do here, all by yourself?"

"I imagine he'll read a good book," Bev sniggered.

Clifford jumped to his feet. He'd had enough.

He glared at Bev.

Bev grinned.

He glowered at Suzie.

Suzie frowned.

"If you'll excuse me," he said indignantly, "I need to go to the toilet." He hobbled back into the hallway and started up the stairs, with a wince of discomfort.

A shuddering Bev looked as if she might pee in her knickers from the laughter that she was trying to restrain. "I guess it's just a one-bed chalet after all, Mrs Williams."

14

With the living room door wide open, Suzie was at the foot of the stairs, gripping the banister and squinting into the unlit alcoves above.

"Cliffy, get back down here!" she howled. "I need you. I need you to go with me. Please, Cliffy."

There was no response to her plea.

She craned her neck in an attempt to spot her elusive husband, who could be lurking in the shadows of the dark landing. But he was nowhere to be seen, and she only succeeded in stretching out her multiple chins; three became two.

Suzie stormed back into the living room and stood over the smirking Bev.

"What did you say to him to make him run off like that?"

"Me! What did *I* say?"

Suzie was incensed. "A regular round at your shop, is he?"

"Yes, he is."

"Bollocks! And you can forget all that crap about lessons in Ribbleton. I know when he's lying." She clenched her fists and took a threatening step toward the vixen.

Bev had the first real inkling of the dangerous situation she was facing. "OK then, I'd like to say that it was nice to meet you, but…well…let's just say it was interesting." With dramatic flair, she drew two thick black lines underneath her scribbles before closing the notepad and returning it to her phoney Dolce & Gabbana satchel. The biro was also put away. She stood up and smiled at her host.

"I think that you—and your husband—have got some issues going on here. Perhaps you should sort them out before you even think about coming to the convention this year."

"You seem to find all this very funny," snarled Suzie. "What's your game?"

"There's no game, Mrs Williams, and in terms of funny, have you looked in a mirror lately?"

"I'm not stupid. I know he's seeing another woman."

"Goodbye, Mrs Williams."

"You're the Sweet Talkin' Woman."

"Whatever." Bev was getting worried for her own safety. It was time to get out as quickly as possible. She tried to squeeze past Suzie without touching her, as if mental illness was contagious.

"Always popping in and out of your shop, is he?"

"Yes."

"What a load of shit! Always popping in and out of you, more like."

"What?"

"It's you, isn't it!"

"What?"

"You and my Cliffy; you've been fucking each other."

"Don't be stupid. He's an old man, and he's gross."

The Spider

"I'm not stupid."

"Look, he comes in our shop for his…oh, for Christ's sake, why don't you ask him yourself, because I've got better things to do."

"You're a slut," hissed Suzie, fists clenching and unclenching.

"What did you say?"

"You're a dirty little slut who prefers older men. Older and married."

"Are you right in the head?"

"No, I'm not, but I'm not stupid either; and I'm not a fucking slut."

"This is pathetic. You are pathetic. Did you know that? You're a total nutjob, and I can tell you that there are no chalets for nutters at my convention." Bev turned toward the hallway. "I'll see myself to the door."

Suzie bent over and picked up the gardening trowel from the coffee table. She gripped it like a dagger. "Oh, no, we can't have that," she growled. "I'll be glad to show you the fucking way out."

15

Clifford sat on the toilet.

He was locked in with the spider, fat and hairy. Big and black, but it was nowhere to be seen.

Now that he thought about it, Clifford couldn't recall whether or not the spider had ever actually existed. A deception designed to support another deception. A lie told so many times that it had become semi-real in the mind of its own inventor.

Clifford's heart sank. His shoulders drooped. His head flopped forward, and he gazed at the magazine that lay upon his lap. Freshly retrieved from his underpants, it was treated with the same reverence that a scholar might show for a Shakespeare First Folio or a Gutenberg Bible.

The naughty nurse on the front cover of this month's *Razzle* was winking at him with 'come to bed' eyes. Despite the pain in his dented penis, the sight of her lacy stocking tops was beginning to stir Clifford's privates. This was the only type of excitement that his deprived nether regions had experienced in recent years, and his hand trembled as he turned over the page to examine the contents list behind the nurse.

Clifford read every word in the introduction blurb for each of the girls who would display their wares on the subsequent pages. When his mouth wasn't open in dumbstruck awe, he mumbled to his glossy harem and occasionally whimpered with wonderment. He was in photographic heaven, and he intended to take his time and relish every second. After all, this was his special treat, his private ritual, and apart from cigarettes, the only thing that kept him sane.

It didn't take long for his manhood to reach its full potential, and he felt the need to unzip and let it see the light. Now with only the one free hand, he continued to peruse the literature that was balanced on his knees.

Big-breasted Jenny on page ten was posing at an airfield. In the first few shots, she was dressed in a long satin gown, but gradually she disrobed whilst climbing the steps into a small private jet, where she completed her strip in the cockpit. According to the write-up about this 'bubbly brunette from Milton Keynes,' she loved to travel.

"I bet she does," Clifford scoffed, "and with knockers like that, who needs a passport?"

The problem with this frequent flyer was that she bore a striking resemblance to Suzie in her glory years, and this made Clifford sad. He could only just remember those mad, marvellous years when Suzie had turned him on with glimpses of her silk lingerie and smutty suggestions on the back seat of the bus into town. This had always led to a bout of vigorous lovemaking behind the bus depot office, or in the bathrooms of the nearest pub, or up against a tree in the local park. He knew that those fantastic days had long since gone, and that they were never coming back. The sudden pangs of sorrow were having a detrimental effect on Clifford's stiffness

The Spider

and, indisposed to lose his momentum, he moved on through the magazine.

Skipping to the last few pages, he frowned at the section entitled "Readers' Wives."

"Lucky Bloody Husbands," sighed Clifford, after several moments of contemplative shaft rubbing, "that's what they should call it."

And now he'd saved his favourite part of the publication for last. It was time to check on the centrefold starlet—Samantha, the sexy nurse.

"Phwoar." Clifford's eyes almost popped out of their sockets as he stared at Samantha bending over a hospital bed and fiddling with a giant syringe. "Oh, my dear God, Samantha, you bad, bad girl."

Resident centrefold Samantha was doing a "Babes in Uniforms" series. Last month, Clifford recalled her as a wayward police officer. "Please come quietly, sir," she had whispered into his imagination.

"Oh, Samantha, I could do without all the other tarts in here, but not you." His right hand moved more vigorously, eliciting that glorious crescendo of sensations. "You are my girl. You keep me going each month. I don't know what I'd do without you," he cooed.

But before he could finish the job in hand, and demonstrate his appreciation for the nurse's hard work, there were three thunderous knocks on the bathroom door.

"Cliffy, we need to talk," shouted Suzie from outside on the landing.

Clifford jerked with surprise, and the magazine fell onto the linoleum floor, pages akimbo. "Jesus Christ, not now," he cursed under his breath.

"Cliffy, is that you in there?"

"Of course it's me. Daft cow! Who else would it be?"

"Cliffy, I know you can hear me," she bellowed.

Masturbatus interruptus is ever so cruel.

There was no way that he could continue with his DIY activities right now. The mood had left him. The urgent fire had gone out. And his unbalanced wife was scratching on the bathroom door. He had no choice but to tuck away his deflating phallus. He picked up the *Razzle* and blew a goodbye kiss to Samantha. He folded her in half and returned the magazine to the waistband of his jeans so that this time it rested snugly in the small of his back. There was no need to hide it behind the boiler just yet. Experience had taught him that Suzie's manic episodes were mostly transient affairs that were easily resolved, and a chance to rekindle his handicraft might come about sooner rather than later.

"Speak to me, you bastard," Suzie squalled. She slammed her fists on the door and rattled its knob.

"What do you want?" Clifford shouted back.

"Open this door."

"No, I'm busy in here."

"Busy, busy, you're always busy in there. What are you doing? This is important."

"I'm having a crap."

"You're full of crap. I could stand here for hours."

The Spider

"For God's sake, Suzie, give me a break. I'll go to your fucking convention; just bugger off and leave me alone for a bit."

"This has got nothing to do with the convention, and you fucking know it."

"I've said I'll go to Ainsdale. Are you deaf?"

"Fuck the convention, Cliffy, just fuck it. I couldn't give a shit about the convention anymore." She thumped the door again. "Open this door."

"Piss off."

A dead calm descended. Had she followed his instruction? Should Clifford pull out his magazine, try to rekindle the mood, and continue with Samantha where he left off? He was suspicious. He listened intently for sounds of movement on the landing that might indicate his wife was shuffling off to fret elsewhere about whatever it was that had agitated her this time. But instead he was shaken by a huge bang as Suzie's foot collided with the door.

"For fuck's sake, Suzie, have you gone totally bonkers?"

"Your little game is over, Cliffy."

"What?"

"Your dirty adventure has come to an end."

"What are you blabbering on about now?" Beneath his angry words, Clifford was getting worried.

"I know all about it."

"Did you take all your medicine this morning?"

"Lessons in Ribbleton. What a load of bollocks; I'm not stupid. I know that things aren't right between us, Cliffy, but I never imagined that you'd be unfaithful. My

God, I was telling her about our sleeping arrangements. She must've loved that."

"Listen, Suzie, I don't know what's gotten into you, but calm down. Go downstairs, and I'll be down in a few minutes to make you a nice cup of tea."

Suzie ignored him and babbled on. "She had a nerve, coming round here bold as brass. What did she expect? She must've been a fucking loony. It's just like in that movie—*Fatal Attraction*—where the loony slut gets killed in the bathroom right at the end." Suzie did well to drag out her memories of the movie. "Yeah, that's right, there's this bit in it where the loony slut comes round to their house pretending to be a buyer or a saleswoman or something. Anyway, she's really there to mix it up with the wife. And then the dirty shagging husband arrives home from work, and he sees her and his face is a picture…just like yours was earlier. Fuck me! It's exactly the same."

"Suzie, what are you talking about? Please try to get a grip."

"But I sussed her out," Suzie said, no longer shouting. Her voice had dropped to a level of creepy calmness, and yet the clarity of her words told Clifford that her lips must have been almost touching the door. "All that shit about 'Remember Freddie'—what a bitch! How could she have used Freddie to lie like that? Cow! Anyway, it doesn't matter anymore. It's all over. She's gone, and Cliffy's stuck in the bathroom instead."

"Suzie, I'm coming out."

16

Rattle and clunk.

The bolt on the toilet door slid back, and Clifford's head popped out. Suzie's face was inches away from his.

"Suzie, I don't know what's wrong with you, but back off and I'll come out."

Suzie waddled backwards so that she was a few feet from the door, and here, in a defiant pose, she stood with her hands on her hips.

Clifford emerged from the bathroom like a naughty schoolboy.

"She's gone, Cliffy, so there's no need to pretend anymore."

"Pretend? Pretend about what?" His eyes were wide with alarm.

"That loony slut of yours has gone; she is no more."

"Slut? Which slut?"

"Which slut! Oh, there's a choice, is there?"

"Suzie, calm down, you're going to burst a blood vessel in your head."

Suzie hopped from foot to foot. She was incensed again, like a toddler having a tantrum, and Clifford's platitudes were only making matters worse.

"Which slut…let me see." She rubbed her double chins and feigned some thoughts before she snapped. "How about the loony one, downstairs! You know—Brian

May's best buddy. Ring any bells yet? The one you've been visiting—no, shagging—in Hardman Street. How could you, you cheating bastard?"

"What! Have you totally flipped? Where's your medicine? Have you taken any of your medicine?"

"You fucking bastard. How could you bring your slut into my house?"

"I didn't bring anybody into *our* house, and as for her downstairs, she isn't *my* slut or *my* anything for that matter."

"Liar!"

"Suzie, we need to call Dr Cassidy right now."

She took a step toward him. "I'm not fucking stupid. I've got eyes. I saw the way you two looked at each other—those dirty, despicable little looks."

"Really, you can see, can you?" Clifford was trembling, and he stepped back so that he was outside the range of his wife's fists. "Well, have you heard yourself? This is total self-deluded shit."

"Her little 'Sweet Talkin' Woman' message; what did that mean? Was it code for something? You're a dirty cheating fucker." Suzie had gone a strange shade of crimson. Sweat oozed from the pores in the furrows of her brow, and she spat a bit of foam as she spoke.

"Stop this!"

"Playing hard to get, Mr Williams," she said, imitating Bev's trill voice, then changing back to her own. "Not hard enough by the looks of things."

"This is all nonsense. Suzie, you're wrong. Stop this nonsense, and calm down."

The Spider

"All that shit about 'Remember Freddie,' but why did she really come round here? I'll tell you why—to look at me, to strut her stuff, and stake her claim on you. Well, I can tell you that I pissed on her fire."

Clifford was worried that his wife was on the verge of a seizure. He took a step back into her fisticuffs range.

"Don't you come anywhere near me, you dirty stinking shagger."

Clifford held out his hand to the woman who, despite everything, he still loved. The only woman he had ever loved.

"Suzie, listen to me. I haven't been with anyone else, sluts or otherwise. You must believe that."

"Liar!" she screamed again. "You haven't been going to give lessons in Ribbleton, have you?"

"Oh, Jesus." He could feel the magazine down the back of his jeans. "This is absurd."

"Always in and out of her shop. What bullshit. Always in and out of *her*. Period."

"No, it's not like that."

"You dirty cheating bastard." Suzie flew at him. With flailing arms, she slapped him and thumped him and scratched at him.

Defending himself, Clifford backed off to the top of the stairs. Not wishing to fall over with the hardcore periodical in his pants, he glanced over his shoulder and failed to miss an incoming right hook. The pain in his jaw jolted him to take drastic action.

"All right, all right, stop this! The truth, I'll tell you the truth."

Suzie suspended her frenzied attack, but she stood ready to resume the assault at a millisecond's notice.

"I know the truth," she snarled.

"No, you don't." Clifford rubbed his jaw. "Do you want to know why I go into that newsagent's shop?"

Suzie was on alert. She was primed for action.

"Do you want to know why I go all the way to Hardman Street and to others over that way? Do you really want to know why I lock myself in the toilet for ages? Do you?"

He lifted up his shirt and pulled out the porno magazine from behind his back. He held it up for Suzie to see.

"What's that?" She was baffled. "Is that a dirty magazine?"

"Yes."

"What—pictures of women with their tits out?"

"You wanted the truth."

For a while, Suzie was confused and speechless, and then she said, "Why have you got a dirty magazine in your trousers?"

"I've been looking at it in the toilet."

"You mean you had a porno magazine with you in the toilet?"

"Yeah, porno magazines, that's all."

"And you've been in there playing with your dirty penis whilst looking at girls in stockings and suspenders?"

"Yeah, all right, I'm not proud of it, but I can assure you that there've been no affairs, no sluts."

The Spider

"No sluts, but what about the bitch downstairs?"

"I don't even know her. She just sold me a few magazines over the last couple of years."

"Over the last couple of years!" Suzie was appalled. "How long has all this wankery been going on?"

"A couple of years or so. I'm sorry, but sometimes I need some…well, you know." He shrugged and looked sheepish.

"No, I don't, so please tell me. Come on, Cliffy, be the big man for a change and spell it out."

"You know, we don't sleep together anymore and—"

"Fuck. If you mean fuck, say fuck."

"OK, we don't fuck anymore, because of your problems."

"Oh, so it's my fault that you're a total wanker, because I'm frigid. Frigid—that's the word you're looking for. Frigid. Go on, say it."

"Suzie, it's not your fault, it's the medicine they keep giving you."

"So to get your rocks off, you've been in my toilet with your disgusting books and pulling your wire."

"But there've never been any real women."

"Beating your meat."

"I swear to you."

"Helping yourself to a hand shandy."

"I love you, Suzie. But for Christ's sake, I'm only human, and I need some relief."

"You disgust me."

"I love you."

"You've cheated on me."

"No, I haven't." He waved the magazine. "This is only pictures."

"Yes, you have. This is still betrayal."

"No, I haven't been with any proper flesh-and-blood women. Please try to understand."

"It's still a betrayal!" she shouted. "You've cheated on me with your mind."

"No, it's just a harmless bit of boob and beaver."

"It's not harmless anymore." Suzie turned to gaze at the stairs and started to cry.

"What do you mean?"

"You've let me down, Cliffy. Let me down with your dirty thoughts."

Clifford followed her gaze. "Suzie, what do you mean? What have you done?"

"You've cheated with your mind. It's mental betrayal."

Suzie wiped the tears from her face and sniffed theatrically. She looked up at her husband and took a purposeful step toward him.

Fearing for his front teeth, Clifford held up his arm to shield his face against any forthcoming onslaught, and he backed away. It was unfortunate that his tiny left foot was not expecting the top step. In the dingy illumination, he misjudged the location of the edge, and his foot failed to cope with the piece of loose carpet.

Stumbling backwards, Clifford clawed at the woodchip wallpaper. He tried to reach out for the finial at the top of the banister. Desperately grasping for it, he found only air. He couldn't recover and let out an unmanly cry for help just before he fell, tumbling

The Spider

away, down the stairs. The magazine fell with him, its pages fluttering around his head—thighs and bums, and boobs and beavers, twisting and gyrating in an airborne display of female flesh. In the half-light of the stairwell, backwards somersaults followed backward somersaults until, with a sickening crunch, the back of his head impacted on the edge of the wall-mounted telephone shelf at the bottom of the staircase.

At least he didn't have to pretend anymore.

17

Clifford lay face down in the hallway, at the bottom of the stairs, unconscious.

Blood poured from a nasty gash behind his left ear, where the fall and the telephone table had combined to do their dreadful damage. His blood soiled the carpet.

On the floor next to his head was the cordless phone handset. Having been off the hook for so long, it was beeping pathetically as if calling out for its cradle, or perhaps crying out to anyone who would listen for help in reuniting it with its other half.

On the other side of Clifford's head was a foot. It was not his foot, but a sad lifeless foot clad in a spangled silver tennis shoe. It was the same size as his girly foot, but it was not his foot. This foot was connected to a dead leg that protruded from the living room door at an unnatural angle. It was Bev's foot.

Suzie was sitting on a step halfway down the stairs and looking down at the mess.

"Cliffy," she whimpered. "Cliffy…Cliffy, can you hear me?"

Neither Clifford nor Bev made any discernable movement.

There was no sound from the carnage below her, except for the beeping of the phone. She was bothered by the phone. It proved to her that other noises apart from her own voice still existed in this nightmare. Or did it? Did this mean that what she was seeing was real, or was it all just another deluded vision?

Suzie shuffled down one step at a time. With each step closer, she stopped and called to her husband; and every time she called, she waited for an answer. But there was none.

At the end of her descent, Clifford was in between her legs, and she leaned forward to push a podgy finger into his left buttock.

"Cliffy, can you hear me? You'd better not be pretending."

Her husband was not pretending anymore, and he said nothing.

Suzie studied the blood-spattered wallpaper and contemplated the circumstances that she found herself in. On most stressful occasions, Clifford was able to offer advice, provide solutions, and sort things out. She felt that this service was only right and proper, as it was he who caused most of her stressful occasions. But now he was no help whatsoever, and Suzie felt lost.

After a while, she stood, stepped over Clifford's body, and rescued the beeping phone from a puddle of blood. Automatically, she put it against her ear to check who was on the line at the other end.

"Hello, can I help you?" She waited and listened to the beep. "Hello, can you hear me?" She was befuddled. "Hello, who's there?"

Disgruntled that no one was willing to speak to her, Suzie snatched up the white plastic telephone cradle and slammed down the receiver. The beeping

The Spider

stopped, and an eerie quietness crept over her. She began to feel alone, a cold and painful loneliness that soaked into her flesh until she felt more alone than she had in years.

Action—that's what was needed; Suzie needed to act. She needed to focus and get on with it…whatever *it* was.

Not quite off the autopilot, she waddled over Bev's corpse and retrieved her gardening trowel from where she had left it—embedded into the side of Bev's neck.

It came out with a pop and a lot more blood. There was always so much blood.

Why was it that, whenever she was so stressed, there was always so much blood?

With insane strength, Suzie gripped Bev under the armpits and heaved the body back through the living room and into the kitchen where it was dumped on the linoleum. It was a sorry sight, and as Suzie leaned against the kitchen table, recovering from her strenuous efforts, she tried to take in the enormity of what was happening. She had murdered someone. She would go to prison. She didn't want to go to prison. She knew that it wouldn't be nice. She suspected that she wouldn't get that special one-on-one care and attention that her husband provided at home. Most likely she'd be beaten by the other prisoners and raped by the guards. Oh no, she couldn't go to prison.

She had to hide the body.

From a cupboard next to the old stove, Suzie pulled out several tea towels. Once they were unfolded, she laid them over the body, starting at the spangled sneakers and working up to the neck, one at a time and slightly overlapping to ensure a total coverage.

She placed one of her favourite paper doilies over Bev's deadpan face. Suzie did this to cover up those dark zombie eyes that might've still been searching this world for the murderer, but also as a mark of respect for the dead. Even a loony slut needs a bit of respect in death.

Satisfied with her work, Suzie closed the kitchen door and trundled back to the hallway, and Clifford. He hadn't moved whilst she'd been away.

She grabbed her mac from a hook on the back of the back of the living room door and put it on. The pornographic magazine and the gardening trowel lay at her feet. She kicked the magazine so hard that it flew across the room and scooted under the couch. Then she picked up the trowel and thrust it into her coat pocket.

On the phone once again, Suzie dialled 999 and waited for a response.

"Ambulance, please." She tried to stay calm and reply appropriately. "Yes, it's 55 Rutherford Road. Yes, it's my husband, he's had an accident. Please come quickly; I think there's something wrong with his head."

18

The little porcelain angel, the one from Suzie's mantelpiece, sat on the bedside cabinet. Broken and haphazardly repaired so many times before, it looked more forlorn than normal.

Clifford lay on the bed, flat on his back. His left leg and arm were in half-plaster, and an oxygen tube protruded from his nose. He was still unconscious. Various sensors were stuck to bare pieces of skin, and their wires fed back to a bank of instruments that bleeped and chirped and whirred whilst several monitors displayed numbers and charts that were incomprehensible to anyone without a medical qualification. His head had been partially shaved and bandaged.

Suzie sat on an uncomfortable plastic chair, a standard issue National Health Service chair, next to Clifford's bed. Her wide eyes were transfixed on her man, and she sang "Bohemian Rhapsody" to him.

"Mama…just killed a man." She was still wearing her mac, buttoned up to her throat, with a bloody trowel in the pocket. "Put a gun against his head, pulled my trigger, now *she's* dead."

Across the ward, in another bed, was another patient with four of his family members gathered around.

As Suzie sang, they looked over at her with concerned disdain. She noticed their attention and broke off from her song.

"What the fuck are you lot looking at?"

Not wishing to make eye contact with a weirdo, they all looked away, except for an elderly gent with a beard. He was disgusted by Suzie's outburst, and he tut-tutted as he left the ward and disappeared down the corridor in search of someone who would deal with his complaint.

Suzie seemed unfazed by their lack of musical appreciation and began a loud rendition of "Killer Queen."

"…dynamite with a laser beam, guaranteed to blow your mind…"

It wasn't long before a staff nurse arrived alongside Clifford's bed. A ward-weary veteran, she had seen it all in her forty years on the front line and was close to a well-deserved retirement.

"Is everything all right, Mrs Williams?"

Suzie ignored her but stopped singing.

A tea break must've ended, or a secret buzzer must've sounded somewhere, or the grapevine must've warned that an inspection by a matron was imminent, because the male surgical ward was now alive with healthcare personnel bustling about in their duties—checking monitors, taking temperatures, moving trolleys, feeling foreheads, and scribbling on flipcharts.

Suzie stared at Clifford and did her best to stay isolated from the hurly-burly. But the old nurse was persistent.

"Mrs Williams…I say, Mrs Williams…Susan, are you OK?"

"Go away."

The Spider

But the nosey nurse did not go away. Instead, she straightened Clifford's sheets. The irritating, fastidious cow.

"Would you like a cup of tea?" she asked Suzie.

"No."

"Has anyone been here to tell you what's happening with your husband?"

"No."

This wasn't true. Only half an hour before, a junior doctor had been round and explained everything, but Suzie couldn't remember it, or the doctor.

"Oh, dear," the nurse sighed, "some of these young doctors get away with murder."

At the mention of murder, Suzie flinched, but the nurse didn't seem to notice and decided to explain herself.

"Apart from a broken tibia, and a fractured humerus, your husband has had a very serious bang on the back of his head. It's this injury that we're particularly worried about."

"Why?" Suzie was listening—perhaps not retaining, but at least she was listening.

"Well, the CT scan—that's the X-ray of Clifford's head that we took earlier—well," the nurse hesitated, "it shows that the bang on his head has caused a bleed under his skull, and the pressure of the blood and fluid is pushing on his brain."

"And?"

"This swelling is causing damage to his brain in that area, and he's going to need an operation to release the pressure, or the damage could be permanent."

"What damage?"

"The thing is that part of the brain is called the visual cortex; it deals with eyesight."

"You mean he's gone blind." Suzie was alarmed.

"Please don't worry. It's too early to say for definite," said the nurse, "but the surgeon needs to operate as soon as possible to limit any damage to your husband's vision that might've already occurred."

Suzie turned to look at Clifford. "Blind!"

"There'll be someone along very soon to prepare him for theatre."

Suzie wasn't listening anymore. As she stared at Clifford, a tear broke away from one of her beautiful doe eyes and rolled down her cheek.

"If you like," the nurse went on, "you can stay here in the waiting room whilst he's in theatre. Mrs Williams…Susan…would you like to do that?"

"No," snapped Suzie, "I've got to go home."

"Oh, I see."

"I've got to take care of someone."

"Your daughter?" enquired the nurse.

"What?"

"Is it your daughter at home waiting for you? Samantha, is it?"

The human mind is a curious thing, and Suzie's took her away to a land of prams and nappies and bottles that never was. "No, we don't have any children," she whispered.

The nurse couldn't hear the dreamy whisper. "Sorry, what was that?"

The Spider

Suzie's gaze dropped to the floor tiles. "We don't have any…" she murmured, "…we don't have any children."

The nurse cupped her hand behind her ear. "I'm sorry, but I didn't quite catch you. What did you say?"

Suzie's head snapped up, and she glared at her tormentor. "We couldn't have children, OK!" she snarled. "Did you hear that? Are you fucking happy now?"

The old nurse was taken aback. "Oh, I'm sorry, but please calm down. I know this is a stressful situation, but you must try to remain calm for everyone's sake." She didn't realise that stress and anger and violence often came as one package where Suzie was concerned. "I meant no offence. It's just that when your husband was brought onto the ward, he was delirious and he cried out for Samantha. I assumed that Samantha was your daughter. I'm sorry, that's my mistake."

Suzie had nothing to say and returned her eyes to Clifford.

The nurse was dismayed. "Right then, anyway, as I said, there'll be someone along in a minute to get Mr Williams ready for surgery."

There was no further response from Suzie, so the nurse left to attend to some other poor souls.

A good ten minutes later, another nurse arrived. Dressed in theatre greens, she was much younger than the previous busybody, perhaps twenty-five. She was slim and pert and cheery. She wiggled in all those feminine places where Suzie found wiggling to be offensive. She picked up Clifford's chart and scrutinised the numbers. During this process, she smiled at Suzie, but her smile was not returned. Suzie eyed the girl with hateful suspicion.

The nurse examined Clifford's bandage.

Suzie didn't like that.

The nurse peeled back one of Clifford's eyelids and shone a pencil light into his pupil.

This agitated Suzie.

The nurse checked out Clifford's other eye.

"Get away from him," Suzie growled.

"I'm just doing my job," chirped the nurse, as she placed her hand on Clifford's forehead.

"Get your fucking hands off my Cliffy, you slut." Suzie stood up.

"Look, there's no need to be rude. I'm sorry, but I've got to get him ready."

Enough was enough for Suzie. She pulled the trowel from her pocket and thrust it toward the face of the girl in greens. The blade, still red with rust and dried blood, stopped millimetres from the nurse's nose. She screamed and ran from the ward.

The family of the adjacent patient was equally startled, and two of them ran after the nurse to fetch help.

By the time a hospital security team had arrived on the ward, Suzie was waving the trowel above her head and howling like a wolf.

"Madam, please put down the weapon," said one of the two uniformed security men. He could hardly believe his eyes as he edged toward the crazed, whirling woman.

The Spider

"Get away from me!" Suzie shouted at the guards and the small crowd of spectators who had gathered to watch from the safety of the corridor. "Get away from my Cliffy, or I'll fucking kill you."

"Madam, please just calm down."

"I will, I'll fucking kill you. I've killed before. Don't mess with me." Suzie didn't want to calm down.

The other guard made a valiant lunge and grabbed her by the trowel arm.

"Help, they're going to rape me!" Suzie screamed, as the two men finally restrained her and then disarmed her. "Help me, Cliffy, help me. Don't let them take me away," she pleaded, as they frog-marched her off the ward. "Cliffy, help me."

Clifford didn't answer her cries for help, and another tiny crack appeared across the chest of the little porcelain angel.